SWIM CRUSH

AN MM SECRET ADMIRER STORY

FINN DIXON

DISCLAIMER

This short story is intended for adult readers only as it contains horny college boys, explicit sex scenes, and graphic language. All sexual activity in this work is consensual and all sexually active characters are 18 years of age or older.

Additionally, Swim Crush is a work of fiction. Names, characters, events and incidents are the products of the author's imagination. Any resemblance to actual persons, living or dead, or actual events is purely coincidental.

It was originally published as a part of the first Candy Hearts Anthology.

CHAPTER 1

My heart felt like it was pounding outside of my chest and my arms were jelly. Coach Sawyer put us through the workout of our lives. Prepping us for the upcoming collegiate championships was his only focus.

"Don't forget to cool down. Good job, boys."

"I need a drink after this. You in, Mike?" Danny asked.

I turned to slap my best friend in the next lane, but he blocked it. "Are you kidding? Wait until after the championships or this might've been for nothing."

Danny didn't seem to like that suggestion, shrugging me off then starting his cool down. I launched myself off the wall in my lane and caught up easily before easing off the throttle.

"I can't hold out much longer," he said, paddling through the water slowly on his back.

Hearing the disappointment in Danny's voice, I suggested, "You could always find a cute fuck?"

"Ha! You're one to talk. What was the point of coming out if you're not gonna find some twink to plow?"

He had been constantly learning new terms to prove how much he supported me. *Twink* was his latest find. His comfort with it made me smile.

"I'm taking my time," I explained as we turned at the wall.

"Don't make me go on Grindr for you. Oh! There's this new app called Stroke. It's for casual stuff like mutual masturbation."

"And Grindr is what? Fancy stuff?" I never thought I would be discussing this with him so openly, but I was so glad we were. "I'm okay, Danny. I can find my own guys."

"Guys he says. You need more than one for it to be plural, and you haven't had any!"

Our conversation continued into the locker room. I nodded and smiled at Hayden, the coach's son, who was talking to Will, one of my teammates, as we entered. Luckily, the rest of the team seemed content to discuss the championships or the latest football scores or whatever else Danny's voice was overpowering.

"Well, what are you looking for? And don't say a relationship."

"Are you gonna let me answer first?"

Danny was always like this. I'd known him since we were kids. Everyone thought we were brothers because we both had brown eyes, brown hair and were inseparable, but he did have a few inches on me.

Height-wise!

Dick-wise, he had a nice one. Despite that whole thing about gay guys being afraid to check out other guys in the locker room, I wasn't like that. I liked dick, so I looked at dick. Plus, he and I kind of fooled around in middle school. You show me yours turned into who could shoot farther.

He was super chill when I came out, which was a bonus. I thought maybe he'd think I was in love with him.

"Earth to Mike! I know you like twinks, so do you want a power bottom or a sub?"

When Danny wanted to learn something new, he really put his heart into it. "You're a walking gay dictionary, you know that?"

"What can I say? I'm an equal opportunity orgasm-enhancer."

Danny wiggled his ass as he left the showers and I followed, thankful that a life's worth of exposure to it had limited my penile response.

Walking back to our lockers, I grabbed a towel from the rack and dried off. It was time to eat and I had a mountain of homework left. A t-shirt and sweats was all I needed. And caffeine.

Before I gathered my stuff for laundry, Hayden was already there.

"Can I get that for you?" he asked.

"Thanks, Hayden. Sure."

He was our equipment manager, and kind of like an assistant coach and whatever else his dad needed him to be. I handed him my towel and picked up my Speedo off the floor where I had pulled it off. Danny handed his towel over, though it left him completely naked. Hayden stuttered something and then disappeared around the corner.

"You didn't have to flash him your dick like that, dude."

Danny ignored me. "What about him? He's kind of cute…in a nerdy way."

"You don't even know if he's gay."

"That's why I gave him the towel. I think he looked. Do you think he looked at it?"

"Jesus, Danny, I didn't notice. I was too busy rolling my eyes at your flagrant display."

"He seems like he'd have a tight ass," Danny said matter-of-factly before pulling up his boxers.

"Shhh! He'll hear you."

"Good, then maybe you'll get laid." He pulled a shirt over his head before adding, "Finally."

"You seem way too concerned about me. What about you?"

"I pulled two chicks last wee– What's that?"

I looked down to where he was pointing. A piece of paper had fallen out of my locker when I pulled my duffel bag out. Even with it on the floor, I could read my name on it. It was folded into a small square, so it took me a second to get to the words.

I think you're amazing, and it means a lot that someone like you is so open and proud about who they are. Like last week, when you wore a different rainbow-themed shirt every day. My favorite was the unicorn one.

It made me feel a little less alone.

With admiration, Harpocrates

"Harpo-what?" Danny shrieked.

I was already Googling it. "The Greek god of silence, secrets and confidentiality."

"Ohhhhh."

"What do you mean, 'Ohhhhh'?"

"You, my friend, have a secret admirer. Looks like I don't have to help you much longer."

Hmmm. I didn't want to get my hopes up too much, but it certainly made me feel good – to have that kind of impact. Even if it was just one person.

CHAPTER 2

"**S**o what did it say exactly?"

My roommate had commandeered homework time as soon as he found out about the note. I should've known better than to mention it.

"Do you still have it?" Logan asked.

"You're as excited as Danny was."

"No shit. He's been trying to get you laid longer than me."

Logan was also comfortable with my homosexuality. Apparently, my pheromones attracted friendly guys that liked being naked around me. I saw Logan's ass more than I saw Danny's. It was a curse and a blessing.

"Both of you have the equipment I'm looking for, so you could've done something about it a long time ago," I challenged, which seemed to shut him up. For a few seconds, anyway.

"Point taken…and let's put a pin in that, shall we? Just show me the note."

Put a pin in that?

His hand was incessant, so I handed it over then asked him to put a shirt on.

"Whatever! I'd be naked if you weren't here all the time."

"You're naked all the time anyway."

He gave up the argument to read the note. "Blah, blah, blah… my favorite was the unicorn one." He paused. "Mikey! The coffee shop! Let's go!"

He grabbed an elastic from his dresser, put his hair up, pulled a shirt on and yanked me out the door before I could even ask why he wanted coffee so late. He'd be up all night and then I'd have to hear him complain about being tired.

He was so excited he had us running to our bikes.

Mack University was a small college, but had a large campus. It took over fifteen minutes to ride from our dorms in the north to the athletic center in the south. But for now, Logan was heading to the cluster of businesses in the center of downtown Brentwood at a dangerous speed, and I was struggling to catch up with him. Coach would kill me if I injured myself doing something this reckless, but Logan was excited. It was hard not to feel the same when he got like this, which, to be honest, was a lot.

When we first met, we were like fire and ice. He was an excitable Golden Retriever and I was a reserved…whatever kind of dog is reserved. I was into sports; he was into the creative arts. I was in the closet; he had two dads. It's not that we were total opposites, but rather complimentary. A fact that helped both of us in more ways than one, but especially academically. He was also the first person I came out to – last year – though when I told Danny next, he wasn't surprised either.

"Come on!" He was jumping up and down at the bike rack. I did not look at the front of his loose shorts.

"Are you not wearing underwear?"

"Were you looking?" I was definitely looking. "Never mind. I already know the answer, and this is exactly why we're here."

What? I was so confused.

He wrapped an arm around my shoulder and led me inside, whispering, "Do you remember last week? It was Pride week and we came here and you ordered an egg-white English muffin with pepper jack cheese?"

"You remembered my order?"

Just like Danny, he ignored me. "The barista – the suave Latino, I think his name was Arturo."

I knew the one he was talking about. He was…handsome. I saw him bend over once. His shirt rode up and the bright teal waistband of his Andrew Christian underwear peeked out, catching my eye. I was ninety-nine percent sure he was gay, and I was a hundred percent sure I wouldn't mind dating him.

"When you went to pick up your order, he said, 'I like your shirt.' Do you remember what one you were wearing? Hmm?"

The uni-

"The unicorn shirt!" Logan triumphantly finished.

He was right. And he was shoving me to the counter to order.

"He's here!" Logan whisper-hissed in my ear, his hand still on my back.

"Uh…"

"Iced white chocolate mocha?"

It seemed the cashier knew my order. "Yeah, that."

"Name?"

"Mike."

Logan ordered and while we waited, he kept pushing me in the back and I kept shushing him. There was no way I was going to say anything to Arturo. He was working.

A few minutes later, his melodic voice called out. "Magic Mike?"

I held in my excitement as he gave me a huge, bright smile. It felt electric when our fingertips touched as I grabbed my drink.

"Thanks." I turned and dodged Logan, who was trying to block my way, picking a booth close to the service counter. I wasn't planning on saying anything, but I could be close enough to stare longingly.

"Why didn't you say anything? You should've slipped him your number!" Logan admonished, sitting across from me.

"Let's use the time we have to help me come up with something to say," I suggested.

"He already likes you. He even gave you a Channing Tatum

stripper joke-name with your drink, *and* he likes your unicorn shirt."

"And he wears Andrew Christian underwear," I added.

"Like your neon jockstraps?"

"Yes, like my neon jockstraps."

"Well, what more do we need to know?" Logan grinned triumphantly. "He definitely plays for your team. I don't see how he didn't write that note."

We proceeded to spend the rest of the evening arguing over the best way to approach Arturo, as if I were offering myself as a virgin sacrifice.

After almost an hour, the last customer left the shop. It was just me and Logan.

"Now's your chance!"

Before I could even get out of the booth, the bell rang above the door. I turned briefly to see a purple-haired pixie of a boy saunter over to the counter.

And plant a big, wet kiss on Arturo's lips.

I simultaneously breathed a sigh of relief and cursed myself for getting my hopes up.

Logan said what I felt. "Guess it's not him then."

"Nope."

"But we *were* right. He does play for your team. Secret admirers usually aren't polyamorous, are they?"

"Don't worry, Mikey. It wasn't Arturo, but we'll figure it out."

Our bikes were stashed again and we were in the stairwell, almost to our floor.

"Maybe I should go by Mike. Mikey sounds like a kid's name."

"Whatever, dude. It's cute."

"Whatever yourself. Nobody calls you Log."

"Well, maybe they will once they've seen it, huh? You know, you have a great ass."

"Your mind is a whirlwind of ideas, Logan, and you just say all of them at once."

I held the door open for him at our landing, letting him take the lead down the hall.

"It's part of my immense charm." Logan soft-punched me in the stomach. "Someone left a note for you!"

My eyes shot to the door and sure enough, there was another note, which Logan grabbed before I could. He shoved it in my hands, and practically yelped, "Open it! Open it!"

I wanted to apologize...kind of. I know the notes are probably creepy, but I don't have your courage. Or muscles.

I'm never this forward. I guess it's the anonymity that's rewarding you with my honesty. I work out but am nowhere near as stacked. I'd ask for workout tips, but how would you get them to me? Lol.

Admiringly, Hercules (aka Harpocrates)

"Wow."

For once, Logan was speechless. I was a little flattered.

I shrugged. "Well, it seems he's noticed my body."

"The *entire school* has noticed your body. You wear practically nothing in the pool." Logan had found words again and unlocked our door. "It's not that hard to notice you're — what'd he say? — stacked."

"He might be too," I said, "though it's a little unclear. He obviously likes mythology. That wasn't just a one-off."

Logan took his shirt off and sat on my bed. "Your powers of deduction are truly staggering."

"Well, I don't hear you coming up with any suggestions!" I

made for my desk chair, remembering Logan's pin comment from earlier. Was he trying to say he was bi?

"Let me think."

I checked my email and socials, then opened my ecology textbook. There was a quiz tomorrow and I hadn't studied much. After a while, I heard a snore and turned to see that Logan was, of course, asleep. *So much for thinking.*

I flipped his covers back, then went over to him. Logan was my height, but a little skinnier, so it wasn't too difficult to move him to my bed.

"Mmm...naked."

He also talked in his sleep. And this had happened often enough that I knew he wanted his shorts to come off. Thankfully tonight, it was a one step process since he wasn't wearing any underwear.

Maybe Logan's your admirer?

He couldn't have put the note on the door. He was at the coffee shop.

After all, he'd just tell me. Plus, when he was naked around me, he was never *hard*. If I were naked around someone I was attracted to, I'd definitely be aroused.

I went down the hall to brush my teeth and take a piss. A bit later, after continuing my daily streak in Marvel's Puzzle Quest and fantasizing about the latest Grindr torsos, I drifted off to sleep, but not before reminding myself to scold Logan tomorrow and make him promise me a favor for having to strip him down again.

The ecology quiz went well. It was mostly about the types of interspecific interactions that structure communities. Commensalism was the one I always got confused, but I studied the fuck out of the recommendations from the TA and lo and behold, it worked out.

When I handed in my quiz, Professor Fraser asked if he could ask me a question. I refrained from the obvious joke – that he already had – and followed him when he motioned to the side of the classroom.

"This is kind of silly, I probably could – well, I know I could – find a personal trainer, but I know you're on the swim team, and well"—he gestured at me—"would you ever consider helping me sometime? Or do you know anybody that could show me around the gym? I've tried to go, but honestly, it's intimidating."

And now that I had a few moments to myself on the way to the dining hall, I had a new theory about my admirer. Professor Fraser *could* be Hercules.

I texted Logan.

I had already agreed to show the professor around the gym since I figured my grade could always use a little insurance. Honestly though, my theory seemed a little far-fetched. Professor Fraser was handsome, but I couldn't imagine he'd use notes to declare romantic interest.

Damn it.

Danny hadn't answered my texts either.

I made my way into the dining hall. It was one of the older ones on campus. You had to descend a wrought-iron spiral staircase to get to the dining area. It was a relic from the seventies and I loved the kitschy architecture. It was also the smallest one, so it was quieter, more intimate. There weren't many students in line, but I did recognize Hayden from behind. He seemed to be by himself.

"Hayden! How's it going?"

He jumped a few inches, then smiled when he realized it was me.

"Sorry, didn't mean to startle you."

"It's fine. I was just lost in my own thoughts, that's all."

"Everything okay?" I asked.

"Honestly? My dog, Aristotle, isn't doing well. I'm just worried."

"Aristotle, huh?"

"Uh…he came with the name."

"Well, at least you can see him. He lives with your parents I'm guessing, right? In town?"

Hayden nodded, then smiled. "Yeah, you're right."

When we both had our food, I asked, "Mind if I sit with you?"

"Sure. I mean, I don't mind."

We found a table in the corner and made small talk about the swim team. I told him what a hard ass his dad was, and he reminded me that he'd spent many more years with him than me. Unable to withstand the need for psychological release, I divulged that Professor Fraser had asked me to work out with him.

"And you said yes?!"

I nodded.

"I wonder if he'll wear tweed in the locker room," Hayden wondered out loud.

"You're kind of funny, aren't you?"

Hayden shrugged. "Better than funny-looking."

I looked down when my phone vibrated. "Finally." I shot off a reply to Danny and told him to meet me at the gym. He didn't know about my second note or the professor.

CHAPTER 3

"Sup?" Danny had found me outside the athletic center, leaning against the wall.

"What took you so long?"

"Jackass. Should I have sprinted here? I didn't think I needed a workout before the workout. We swimming, lifting, or both?"

I shrugged. "Maybe both. Start with weights? Also, by the way, Logan and I found a second note." I fished it out of my pocket and let him read it. "Thoughts?"

"Well, he likes Greek mythology-"

"Also, Professor Fraser asked me for workout tips today." I held the door open for him.

"You think a professor would hit on you?"

"Shhh!" There were a few other people in the foyer.

"Or leave a note in your *gym* locker?"

"I don't know. It's not like this has happened before."

"We can keep trying to figure it out, but I reckon he's just building up the courage to tell you in person."

"What makes you say that?" I didn't see anyone changing or in the showers as we walked to our lockers.

"The comment about working out. The whole tips thing. You have no way of talking to him."

"True."

I pulled my tank and shorts out of the bag and a note fell out. Danny grabbed it before I could even say something. He read it out loud.

> *I'm probably coming on too strong, but I've known you long enough that I'm sure we'd get along. My favorite color is green as well. You swim faster every time you wear your green speedo, by the way.*
>
> ♥ *Hermes*

"A heart this time, and another Greek name. Messenger of the gods because…"

"It's another message," I finished for him, stating the obvious.

"Cheeky."

"And it seems he's watched me swim…a lot."

"I'd be flattered, Mikey, and if I were gay, I'd be all over you. Everyone on the team has a great body, but you've also got a handsome face and great hair."

"So you're Hermes?" I deadpanned, stripping off my clothes.

"Look at you. You have no shame either. You just flop it around everywhere."

"It's right here." I pointed to my dick. "It can hear you."

"Well, your jock's right here." He tossed it at me. "Put it on! Logan and I are a bad influence on you."

"I hope my admirer, or any future boyfriends, like porn as much as I do because I see enough real life peen that it almost doesn't affect me anymore."

"I'm so sad this doesn't do it for you."

I glanced his way, and of course Danny was the naked one now. It wasn't that he wasn't hot. I just learned a few years back it was pointless to lust after straight guys. The ones that were super chill around me naked felt different anyway. It wasn't erotic; it was just a body.

Now if Logan or Danny were more touchy-feely, then that would be different, and I'd have to tell them to stop if they didn't want me to maul them. I was a closet cuddler, but I theorized cuddling was just a gateway to sex. I'd only ever find out once I tried it, but that felt like what would happen.

"Ready?" Danny asked.

"Let's go."

"What about Ethan?" Danny asked, trailing behind me.

"No."

"Andy?"

"No."

"Will?"

"For the last time, Danny, I don't think anyone else on the team is gay." We entered the locker room together after an hour-long ass-kicking weightlifting session. We both worked so hard, it was impossible to play love detective, but now that we could breathe again, Danny was back on the case.

"Well, if y'all are ten percent of the population, and there are twenty guys on the team, statistically, there *has* to be another gay dude."

"Think about the notes again. He saw me in my pride week shirts. He knows I'm muscular."

"Anyone with eyes knows that."

I continued, "He's been to our swim meets and knows I like the color green."

"*Are* you faster when you wear your green Speedo?"

"I have no idea, Danny. I've never noticed a connection before."

"Well, what color do you have today?"

I grabbed my bag and opened it. I couldn't remember. "Pink."

"Oh well."

"What do you mean? We're doing a cool down swim. Even if I had the green Speedo today, cool down doesn't mean swim as fast as I can."

"Whatever." Danny was naked again. "Wear the green one at the next meet. Hermes obviously believes it's true. Maybe it is?"

I changed into my Speedo and we headed to the pool. "How many laps?" I needed to clear my head. These notes had me all over the place.

"I dunno. Twenty?"

"Sounds good."

Danny had a student government thing, so I found myself alone for dinner, preparing myself for tonight's session with the chemistry TA. I was better with concepts than concrete principles, so I was getting all the help I could since it was basically science-math. Ecology was doable; organic chemistry was hell.

I liked to get there early, so I scarfed down the rest of my tacos as fast as I could and scurried over to the science building. It was one of the oldest buildings on campus, so there were lots of little nooks and crannies for studying. Sam, the chemistry TA, always had us meet on the third floor at the back since it was only a few hundred feet from his lab. I didn't pretend to be smart enough to know what he was working on.

It's not that I liked chemistry that much, but I had noticed that the closer you sat to Sam, the more help you received. It was a theory, but one I was unwilling to test. I needed the help, so I always sat close.

I don't think he was doing it intentionally. It just happened that way.

I took the stairs two at a time, using the old wooden banister to keep my balance. It was one of the few buildings with carpet, so it helped keep it quieter than anywhere else. Plus, with the smaller spaces, there just wasn't a lot of room for things to echo.

"Hey, Cap, good to see you."

Sam, of course, was already there.

"Cap?" I took the seat to his right.

Sam kind of grimaced. I wasn't sure what to make of it, until he said, "Sorry, you kind of remind me of Chris Evans. You have this whole all-American corn-fed white-boy vibe – not that I should've said that – but he played Captain America."

"I got there once you said Chris Evans…and thanks? I think."

"Trust me. It's a compliment."

Well, well, well. Sam had just moved into the lead as the anonymous admirer. It was hard to ignore a come-on that strong.

I knew it was a compliment. If I ever met Chris Evans, I'd have a hard time forming a coherent sentence let alone resisting the urge to strip, bend over, and wink at him.

Not that I felt like a bottom, but for him, I'd do just about anything.

I felt the tension between us build, the heat radiating off his leg, which had brushed mine when I sat down. He licked his lips, then glanced at me, meeting my stare. I hadn't stopped looking at him since he said it was a compliment. He had a flawless jawline, accompanied with a little bit of scruff. It certainly wouldn't be a detriment to be with an older guy for my first time. I'm sure Sam had more experience than me.

"What?" he asked.

I took my chance, grabbing the back of his neck and pressed my lips against his. I started to probe with my tongue – that's what you're supposed to do, right?

"Whoa!" Sam pulled back, out of my grip, and wiped his lips with the back of his hand. "Is it like a TikTok trend to kiss a straight guy and see his reaction?"

Straight guy?

"Fuck, I'm so sorry." I felt the heat rush to my face. "You're straight?"

"It was the nickname, wasn't it? I should've kept my mouth shut. I thought you'd just be flattered. I have a nickname for everyone. They're not all nice ones." He chuckled, but all I could think about was how fast I could run away. Right now. "And yeah, I have a girlfriend."

He must've seen the six thousand emotions on my face.

"But kudos to you for having the balls to do that, man!"

I couldn't sit here. I was mortified.

"Don't go!" He grabbed my arm as I stood up, which gave me pause. "It's fine. I mean, it's not that it was a bad kiss. It was just a misread, right?"

Truth be told, I needed help with the course. I couldn't academically afford to leave, so I explained. "I'm glad to hear it. I-I don't have much experience. It's just…I've had these anonymous notes…from a secret admirer."

"You're kidding me."

I pulled the latest one out and showed him. It made him smile.

"Makes a little more sense now. I'm assuming you thought I might be a candidate?"

I nodded. "It's someone that knows me well and takes note of what I wear. I dunno. You dress well, and then the Chris Evans thing. I was probably imagining half of it."

"More like all of it?"

I practically died when he said that, but once I saw his expression, it was clear he was joking.

But I must've still been giving off mortified vibes.

"I'll be honest, Mike. If I was into guys, you'd be at the top of my list. Does that make you feel better?"

At this point, other people had shown up and I just wanted to crawl under a rock and forget this happened. I didn't need the entire study group to know that I had launched myself lips-first at Sam.

Logan and Danny were going to laugh their asses off when they found out about this.

That is, *if* they found out about this. I certainly wasn't going to tell them.

Okay, maybe I'd tell them. After all, I was all out of ideas as to who the mystery Greek aficionado could be.

CHAPTER 4

Logan never came back to our room. I wasn't quite sure where he was, but after dinner, homework, and a shower, I didn't necessarily mind having the room to myself. Logan's lack of shame vis-à-vis nudity also extended to self pleasure. And while I was comfortable being naked in a locker room and slightly less so in my dorm room, I wasn't quite at the point where I wanted to jack off with Logan ten feet away.

But at the moment, I didn't have to worry, so I took the opportunity to get naked under the comforter and open Grindr. Even though it was a small university, there were plenty of nearby distractions. And while I wouldn't drive as far as Nashville for a hookup, their bodies still looked as nice.

After all, I could only embarrass myself so much with this secret admirer business before I needed to change universities. Right now, my hand and some explicit banter with the headless torso of a stranger would be enough.

Before I could even pick a guy to chat up, the blip came through, so I clicked on my messages.

SmoothTwink19: Hey. Looking to deepthroat and swallow. You available?

SmoothTwink19 was headless, but indeed smooth. He had the kind of body I would get behind and rail. In theory. I said a silent thank you to whomever was responsible for providing me with tonight's entertainment and started typing.

> CircusTent: I'm not sure you can handle it.

> SmoothTwink19: I've got a big mouth.

I laughed at his spunk. It seemed I liked an agreeable bottom and my dick did too. It was moving slowly, in an arc, sweeping over the top of my thigh as it hardened. I shivered as the head brushed against the stubble that had started to grow in. It was almost time to shave again; we had a meet this weekend.

> CircusTent: That's not the only hole I'm interested in.

> SmoothTwink19: Let's see what you got.

Not gonna lie. I had an album of ready to go pics and my go-to was a post-shave shot where my dick looked enormous. I was seven and a half, larger than average.

The three Europeans on the swim team thought it was strange that the rest of us knew our dick sizes. It turned out they had never bothered to measure. Before coming to America, no one had ever brought it up, which we all found hilarious because we had all played some form of show-me-yours in grade school.

It seemed only natural to me after all since we'd spent enough time with each other naked. Eventually someone threw a boner and the conversation became a bragging contest, but it didn't really matter. There was only one guy bigger than me on the team – Jamie, aka Thermos. He wasn't the fastest on the team and we all knew why. It was a joke, of course, but one that he didn't mind.

> SmoothTwink19: Fuck. I want that inside me now.

SmoothTwink19: You on or off campus? Can you host?

Straight to the point. A little desperate, but I wasn't looking to hook up. I just wanted to jack off.

Poor guy.

CircusTent: You getting that hole ready for me?

I got another blip, so I clicked over. It was habit. Smooth-Twink19 wasn't going anywhere, and my dick wasn't getting soft any time soon either.

PillowByter: Hi Mike, good to know you're a "big top". ;)

Okay. How the fuck does this person know it's me?

PillowByter: I know how you like puns, and I recognize your chest.

PillowByter: You have freckles in the shape of Orion on your left pec.

PillowByter: And I like Greek myths.

PillowByter: I'm your secret admirer btw.

Ohhh.

Interesting…and ballsy.

CircusTent: I'd almost be terrified if I wasn't already turned on.

There was a pause, and I wondered for a second if I said some-thing wrong.

PillowByter: You can't say things like that, Mike.

CircusTent: What did you expect? This is Grindr, babe.

PillowByter: *melts*

CircusTent: How do I know this isn't Logan or Danny giving me shit?

PillowByter: I guess you'll just have to figure that out on your own.

A part of me – the still horny and hard part – took over.

CircusTent: I'm assuming a big top does it for you, especially if you're biting the pillow.

CircusTent: Is arched and on all fours your natural position?

PillowByter: For someone like you, I'd do whatever you wanted.

Fuck.

PillowByter: Was that what you wanted to hear?

Now, I wasn't sure if he was just saying that or if that's what he actually wanted.

CircusTent: Are you trying to confuse me?

PillowByter: You're a smart guy. Figure it out.

And then the most perfect photo I'd ever seen came through.

His ass was like a porcelain sculpture, better than anything I'd seen in porn. If it ended up being real and I was ever in its presence, I'd make it feel so good. I could feel the precum starting to ooze onto my stomach.

> CircusTent: Is that an invitation?

PillowByter: I wish! Why do you think all the notes and now this?

PillowByter: I might be a flirt, but I'm shy as fuck.

> CircusTent: So you show me your perfect ass and now you're shy? I don't buy it.

PillowByter: So it was perfect?

> CircusTent: Fuck, yes.

PillowByter: Good to know your weakness.

PillowByter: I showed you mine…

Cheeky bastard.

> CircusTent: You already know I'm stacked. :-P

PillowByter: I've seen a lot, but now you have something to use as your phone's wallpaper and all I have are memories.

His sense of humor was definitely a match for mine. Before I could respond, more messages came through.

PillowByter: But maybe I should've left a little more mystery?

PillowByter: I don't want you to think I'm easy.

PillowByter: Good night, Mike.

What? Wait!

Before I even hit send, I knew that he was already offline. I scrolled back up to his butt and resumed stroking. The idea that he knew who I was based on my body was fucking hot. Sure, it was a little stalkery, but he was funny, he was flirty, and his ass was magnificent. It wasn't like he had a lock of my hair in a neck-lace or anything.

Probably not?

I was close, so I draped a t-shirt on my stomach and pulled up some twink getting double-teamed on Pornhub on my phone to finish.

After Pillow's forwardness, it didn't take long. As I groaned and bucked, the cum shot out of my dick onto the shirt. With each spurt, I felt more satisfied and warm and smiley.

The gods of masturbation must've been watching out for me because as soon as I wiped up and tossed the shirt on the floor, the door opened. The beam of light from the hall illuminated the entire room. Logan was back.

"Hmm, howdy sailor, smells like someone just had a wank in here."

I was loath to answer but did. "It smells like that all the time."

"I knew you were still awake."

I heard him moving through the dark. "Yeah, don't worry about it. Just me trying to sleep here."

"Riiight."

"Where the fuck have you been anyway?" I asked.

His bedside light turned on and I looked over to see him pull his shirt off.

"I was studying."

"Without any books?"

"They're all digital now." Off came the shorts.

"It was that embarrassing?"

"You wouldn't believe me if I told you."

"I thought you were studying."

He looked over at me with a grin. "It was a hookup, alright? Let's leave it at that."

I did not want to hear about whatever girl or girls he messed around with, so I kept my words to myself and continued to watch the show I knew he was putting on for me.

Though I wasn't gonna keep my mouth shut about that. "You know you can get undressed with the lights off, right?"

He turned, pulled his tighty whities off, giving me the full view, and said, "Where's the fun in that?"

Bastard knew I'd watch. He liked the attention, and who was I to keep it from him?

I had never met a more average straight guy than Logan the day we moved into the dorms, but it only took a week for the real Logan to emerge. Naked, of course.

"So tell me about your evening? Did you wait up all night for me to come home, dear?"

"My secret admirer messaged me on Grindr."

"What?!"

So I told him what happened, and then he wanted to see PillowByter's ass. I didn't want to send it to him, so he got out of bed and walked over to stare at it on my phone.

"Nice!"

"You know, some days I question your sexuality."

"Nudity doesn't have anything to do with sexuality, Mikey. Plus, I believe that everyone should be proud of their bodies, and I'm not ashamed of mine."

"Clearly."

Logan went back to his bed, but left the light on. "So are you going to message him?"

"He's offline *and* he's my secret admirer. He'll contact me when he's good and ready."

"I'll bet you're good and ready after that photo."

"I finished before you arrived."

Logan laughed and then kept laughing. "I'm not surprised."

And then we talked about swimming and his weird anthropology professor and how he sometimes thought about which Disney movie he'd want to live in.

At some point, he shut the light off and we both fell asleep.

CHAPTER 5

met Professor Fraser, who told me to call him John, at the gym and started by giving him a tour of the facilities. I noticed his sneakers and told him they were mostly for running and that if he wanted to get serious about weightlifting, cross trainers would be better since they were more multi-purpose.

"So I need new shoes?" He looked confused.

"I didn't mean to overwhelm you. I'll send you some links for what I'm talking about."

I started him off on an arms and abs workout, and explained I hit the gym five times a week and targeted different areas of my body each session. I tried to make it sound simple but I was afraid it was still too complicated.

"I promise it'll get easier."

"I hope so. You really don't mind doing this?"

I shook my head. *Not if it helps my grade.*

While he worked out, I recalled the image PillowByter sent me. Surprisingly, I wasn't caught staring at his ass, but after a few good looks, I was fairly certain it wasn't a match. The professor was handsome, but his butt was not as plump as the one in the photo.

"Don't you have swim practice?"

"Not for another hour."

An hour later Danny was as excited as Logan had been.

"I can't believe your luck, you son of a bitch. Secret letters and then a nice, juicy peach. Maybe if I rub your head, some of it will rub off on me."

I ignored the innuendo and humored him, letting him rub my head while I grabbed my body wash and headed to the showers.

"Nice job, gentlemen," Coach Sawyer said, walking in from the pool. "I know the championships are still months away, but we've got plenty to do before then. It's full steam ahead."

I snuck past Coach and headed to the shower head closest to the door.

The door opened again and Hayden came through carrying a stack of towels.

"And the holidays are coming up, so...everything in moderation."

"Don't forget about the friendly, Dad."

"Oh shit, I mean, yeah. Thanks, Hayden. Right. We had a few private high schools approach us and propose a friendly meet between their teams and us this weekend." He ignored the groans. "It's good PR for us, guys, and I'm well aware – as they are – that we are extremely likely to win every event, but it's good practice for them. It's this Sunday. Hayden will send out the meet program with assignments before the weekend."

I glanced at Hayden. He was wearing a tanktop – it was warm in the gym after all. I had never noticed his arms before, but damn. I'd never seen him in the pool, but he must do *something* to keep those muscles. He met my gaze.

I'd been caught checking him out but didn't want it to seem that way, so I slowly turned to face the water. Another pump of body wash and I reached to lather my ass...which I...just practically shoved in Hayden's face by turning around. *Shit!* Did he think I did that on purpose? I couldn't turn around *now*, so I dipped my face into the stream and got my hair wet. Turning around again, I leaned back, letting the water pull the hair off my forehead, and wiped my eyes clear.

Hayden was gone. I breathed a sigh of relief. That would've been something! My bare naked ass checking him out...totally appropriate.

"Earth to Mr. Ramsey!"

"What?"

"I know you have a lot going on, but as your best friend, I'm insulted." Danny glared at me from the shower head next to mine.

"Well, spit it out. What'd I miss?"

"How are you not glued to your phone?" Danny asked.

"What do you mean?"

"You've got a guy with an amazing ass that worships you at your fingertips and you're spending precious minutes soaping up your body with us water jocks."

I shrugged and smiled. "It's not so bad here, you know."

Danny rolled his eyes. "You've seen all our dicks like a hundred times. Plus, we're like brothers. Unless you're into that sort of thing?"

"Uh, no. I have a brother and that's- Wait, would you do your brother if you were gay?"

"Who's doing their brother?" Ethan asked.

"Is Mike going on and on about being gay again?" Andy teased.

"Danny started it!" I said like an adult.

"You two should just fuck and get it over with," Will added.

"No one is fucking anyone in here!" Coach popped his head out of his office. "Hayden! Shut the hot water off, they should all be clean by now."

The team rushed to rinse off whatever soap was left. Half of them teased Hayden to disobey his father's command and the other half shut off the water and ran to the lockers. Danny and I were in the latter group.

In the rush to get out, the team knocked over the pile of towels Hayden had left for us. As the other guys swarmed around us, Danny and I gathered what we could off the floor just as Hayden reappeared.

"You didn't really shut the hot water off, did you?" Danny asked.

"No," Hayden whispered, "but don't tell my dad."

I stood up and Hayden's eyes widened.

"Here ya go, cowboy." Danny slammed a towel into my stomach. "You'll poke his eye out with that thing."

"I-I…" I didn't know what to say. While picking up the towels, I sprouted a boner and Hayden had seen it. *Fuck.*

"Can't take you anywhere," Danny mumbled as he pulled me away from a still speechless Hayden.

Back at the lockers, Danny asked, "What the fuck was that? Towels get you excited now?"

"I don't know. It must've been the friction when I knelt down to pick them up."

"Dude, you *need* to open Grindr and work your magic on that guy if towels are starting to float your boat."

Danny was half-dressed and I was sitting on the bench, still in shock at exposing myself like that in front of Hayden. He must've noticed I was frozen.

"Hey, don't feel that bad. Hayden's seen us all naked before and I've popped a stiffy or two in odd places."

"Oh yeah? Where?"

"Um…"

"You're such a liar." Finally, muscle memory returned and I went through the routine of drying off and dressing.

"The school bus!"

"The school bus?"

"Yeah, it used to bounce around on the dirt roads. Instant tumescence."

"I see that your Word of the Day calendar is paying off, but you were like thirteen. Ravioli probably made your dick hard."

"Whatever! The point is friction is friction. So you waved your fully engorged wank wand in front of another guy. It's not like you jizzed all over him or anything."

"He looked stunned."

"It *is* almost eight inches. Stunned is an appropriate response, is it not?"

Flattery wasn't going to make me feel better. "Should I apologize?" I pulled my briefs up and tossed the towel aside.

"Mike, you should just drop it. It's over. Bringing it up again would only make him uncomfortable."

"You think he was uncomfortable?"

"Probably? I mean, it isn't every day a guy gets a hard dick in the face, is it?" Danny laughed. "You'd like that, but I don't know about Hayden."

"You know I can hear you guys, right? This locker room is like an echo chamber."

Shit! Shit! Shit!

It was Hayden. He came around the corner, grabbed our towels, and said, "For what it's worth, I am gay, but I've seen better." And with a wink, he walked away.

If embarrassment could kill someone, I'd be dead. I looked through my fingers, horrified, to see Danny's mouth and eyes wide open. He was as stunned as I was.

It's all we could talk about on the walk back to the main campus.

After saying goodbye to Danny, I made my way up the stairs. The warmth of the building made me realize how cold I was. It was time to break out my hoodie. Clearly, winter was coming.

I opened the door to-

"I'm cumming!"

-find Logan blasting a rope of dick sauce all over his stomach.

"Jesus Christ!" I turned away, but it would be forever

ingrained in my memory. "There wasn't a sock on the door. We agreed to put a sock on the door!"

"Is someone there? Turn the camera off!"

From my seat on the bed, I could hear Logan fumbling with something before he said, "Later, babe," then, "Dude, that was shit timing."

"Tell me about it. I did not need to see that," I replied, which only reminded me of what happened earlier. After all, Hayden didn't need to see what I had shown him. "Do I need to bother asking their name or was it a one time thing? And since when do you have cam sex?"

"Less mess."

With what I had seen, I doubted that. "Do you need a minute to clean up? Should I leave?"

"No."

I flopped onto the bed, facing the wall and opened Grindr.

"I'm sorry I didn't put a sock on the door, Mike."

"Apology accepted." I sighed. It didn't look like PillowByter was online.

"I'm decent. You can look now."

I flipped onto my back and chanced a look Logan's way. "Really?"

"What?" He shrugged.

"A crop top and denim cutoffs? It's almost November *and* it's not nineteen eighty-three."

"One, we're inside. Two, the eighties were amazing. And three, it's a cropped football jersey."

"Where'd you get a cropped football jersey and why?"

"Ebay," he answered, "and don't judge me! Chicks like it. Makes me look like a jock. Do you like it?"

I rolled my eyes, but begrudgingly had to admit the attraction. "You know I'm madly in love with you, Logan. Clothes that showcase your fantastic abdominals are a blessing."

"Shut the fuck up. I know you love all this." He rubbed his stomach for emphasis, which made me smile.

"Your humility really adds to it." I changed the subject. "Is this thing"–I gestured to his computer–"serious?"

"As serious as you and PillowByter," Logan answered.

"That's vague. Was this your first time?"

Logan laughed. "No, we've done this a few times."

Another coy answer. I was fine with him keeping secrets. It's not like I told him everything. I certainly wasn't going to tell him about awkwardly waving my boner in Hayden's face today.

CHAPTER 6

"Oh God." I murmured as I approached Danny. We were in between heats, keeping warm in oversized team hoodies.

"What?"

I grabbed him by the elbow and steered him into a corner where we wouldn't be overheard. There was enough noise in the natatorium anyway. The meet against the local high schoolers was well underway.

"What is it? You're scaring me."

"What if PillowByter is one of these guys?"

"One of what guys?"

"The high schoolers!" I hissed, still clutching his arm.

Danny laughed at me. "None of these guys would have the balls to do that. They're kids."

"Hilarious, Danny, and untrue. Some of them are eighteen, maybe nineteen, and one of them just said he liked my Speedo. I said thanks, walked a few steps, then turned around. I caught him staring at my ass."

Danny shrugged. "It's a great ass."

"Be serious!"

"So what if it's one of these guys? Take the compliment that someone would go out of their way to make you feel good about yourself. Both PillowByter and the random toddler that just checked out your ass."

I tried not to pout, but Danny was not seeing how awkward this would be.

"Hey, I don't want to be sitting on your porch fifty years from now sipping unsweet iced tea and hear you whining about how you wish you got more ass in college. Eighteen year-old ass is still ass."

"Now that's a bumper sticker." I took a breath, trying to calm down.

"I'm serious, man. Have a fit when you find out it's an eighteen year-old. No use having one now. He's probably someone that's right in front of your nose and you don't even know it."

I tried to ignore the feeling that it *was* one of the random nearby teenagers.

"Where'd you get that Speedo?"

I turned to find a rather tall boy smiling at me. A glance told me he was from Smithfield Academy and before I could answer, he pulled off his swim cap and shook out his wavy brown hair. It was almost down to his shoulders.

"Green's my favorite color. Wish we didn't have to wear the school's colors. Navy blue is so drab."

I answered, "I actually got this online. International Jock, I think."

"It suits you."

I elbowed Danny beside me. He had started giggling.

"I'm Tom, by the way." He held out his hand.

"Mike. This is Danny." Danny, who had finally quieted down, shook his hand as well. "Enjoying the meet?"

"It's getting better."

I was looking at the pool, but with my peripheral vision, I could tell he was smiling. And staring. At me.

"I don't do this often, Mike, but would-"

"Hey Mike," Hayden said, popping up out of nowhere, "Coach wants to see you."

Thank God.

"Ten-four," I replied before shooting Tom a smile. "Nice to meet you, Tom. Good luck with the rest of the meet."

I left Tom with Danny and Hayden. He was cute, but despite Danny's coaxing, I was not about to go on a date with someone in high school. Even if they were taller than me.

I quick-stepped over to Coach. He was busy chatting with a few older gentlemen, presumably, the other coaches. Standing slightly off to the side, it seemed I wasn't as noticeable as I thought.

"What is it, Mr. Ramsey?"

I was caught by surprise, but managed to explain that Hayden sent me over.

"Did he now? I can't imagine why."

"So, you didn't need to see me?"

"If I did, I forgot the reason."

"Is this your best swimmer, Sawyer?" one of the other coaches asked before I could leave.

Coach's arm wrapped around my shoulders and pulled me closer to the group. "That's right."

"Mind if I grab him for a few minutes to help out our best guy. He's the anchor for our relay."

"Mike's a good sport, aren't you, Mike?" Coach Sawyer slapped my back, causing me to jump, but I smiled and nodded.

"Sure thing, Coach."

"Tom! Come here for a sec!"

I closed my eyes, took a breath, and willed it to not be the tall underage glass of water named Tom from earlier.

"How was Tom?" Danny asked.

We'd left the meet without showering, and it was mostly

because I didn't want Tom and his friends getting an eyeful of me in the shower. Under normal circumstances, I wasn't ashamed of my nude body, but during my time "helping" Tom out, it was almost embarrassingly clear that he was smitten. It became abundantly clear when he handed me a note – *a note!* – with his number on it.

"Aroused and confident. I could see *it* filling his Speedo and then he gave me his phone number."

"I still think it's nice."

"It is nice, but it doesn't mean anything." I continued listing the ways it was never going to work, but after a few minutes with no response from Danny, I checked to see what he was doing. He was on his fucking phone. "Something more important than my sex life?"

"Oh, stop whining. I'm looking him up." He waved his phone in my face. "Tom Cockburn. He was born September twentieth, making him just over eighteen."

"Where'd you find all that?"

"Smithfield Academy's website," Danny answered.

"Detective Danny," I said before looking both ways.

We crossed the street and headed northwest towards the best dining hall on campus. I was always starving after a meet, even a friendly.

Blip.

"Grindr calls," Danny said.

"I still love that you can recognize that sound. Wonder if it's PillowByter."

"Well, let's not leave us in suspense too long. Whip it out."

The phone recognized my thumb, and then it was just a swipe and a tap. "It's him!"

"Jesus! They probably heard you in the library."

I shoved Danny and clicked on the message.

PillowByter: You did great today.

PillowByter: Seemingly popular with the younger men of the region.

Before I could ask-

PillowByter: I was jealous.

"Damn, Mikey, he was at the meet!"

I felt my heart rate increase. The thought of being watched was strangely erotic.

Danny continued, "I doubt he was one of the high schoolers. He would've said peers instead of younger men."

I considered that for a second and had to agree. Partially because I wanted it to be true.

CircusTent: Does that mean you're my age?

PillowByter: I can tell you I'm not in high school.

I breathed a sigh of relief.

PillowByter: I'll be in high school next year.

"Oh shit, I like this guy." Danny, who was reading next to me, chuckled.

CircusTent: I'm a little young for someone to call me Daddy, but I can try it.

"Ooh, you're better at this than I thought you would be."

"And why is that?" I asked.

"Because you're a virgin," Danny whispered.

"I can still have a sense of humor. Plus, I've seen so much porn. You pick these things up."

"Ah yes, the Schlong School of the Arts. How could I forget Professor Power Bottom and his teaching assistant, CumPig?"

It was my turn to chuckle. "Do you mind?"

Danny backed off. "Keep me abreast of any developments. I'll be over here on Tinder."

PillowByter: You're too hot to be a dad.

PillowByter: I'm kidding. I'm your age.

CircusTent: I figured/hoped.

PillowByter: I'll be honest.

PillowByter: I haven't stopped thinking about what it'd be like to get fucked by you.

Holy fuck.

I reached into my sweats and adjusted my hardening dick. PillowByter was horny and making me even more so. I weighed going to eat versus heading back to the dorm for an intimate session with my growing cock.

"Do you need a few minutes?"

"Huh? What?"

"Are you going to eat with me or are you going to hit the bathroom and jack off first?"

I sputtered, trying to think of a reply, but Danny continued.

"I can wait if you need a few minutes."

"No, that's alright."

CircusTent: Will you be around in an hour or so?

CircusTent: This conversation is causing a disturbance in my pants that isn't appropriate for public consumption.

PillowByter: Oh really?

PillowByter: I'll admit it's easier to flirt with you this way than in person.

CircusTent: Have you ever flirted with me in person?

"Watch out for the pole!"

Whoa! Danny yanked me sideways, just as I glanced up and

saw the street lamp flash in front of me.

"I guess I should probably put the phone away while I'm walking," I said.

"You think?" Danny shook his head and smiled.

As soon as we sat down with our food, I pulled my phone back out.

> PillowByter: I'm not sure our interactions count as flirting.

I showed Danny the message.

"Well, that proves he is in front of your nose."

I groaned. "I wish he'd reveal himself."

Danny laughed, and then I realized what I said and joined him.

"Oh please, you like the attention, Mike."

I considered that while I took a bite of grilled chicken. "Fine. I can admit it's been fun."

> PillowByter: I can be on later if that's easier for you.

> CircusTent: It's a date.

Shit.

Danny must've seen my face, so I showed him. "So what? It kind of is a date."

"You don't think I just fucked it up?"

"The dude sent you a photo of his ass and wrote three love notes, I don't think he's going to care if you use that term."

> PillowByter: Sounds good.

Whew.

CHAPTER 7

t turned out using that term was fortuitous.

Because it led to PillowByter suggesting bi-weekly chats which continued over the holidays.

For Thanksgiving, we had both stayed on campus, but for Christmas, he stayed and I flew home. I tried to deny it, but my siblings could tell something was up. My older brother kept telling everyone I had finally found a "special boy". After he asked in private if I had given my flower away yet, I introduced my fist to his stomach and since my bicep was twice the size of his, he didn't ask again.

PillowByter wouldn't reveal why he stayed on campus for Christmas, and I didn't push him about it. There were plenty of reasons, and they weren't any of my business. Especially if he didn't want to share.

The fact that we were miles apart didn't matter. In every conversation, with each passing message, I felt closer to him. That should've been weird, but it wasn't.

PillowByter: Did Santa bring you anything amazing?

CircusTent: No jockstraps. Sad face.

PillowByter: That is sad.

PillowByter: You'll just have to send a nude instead.

CircusTent: Did Santa bring you anything for your junk?

PillowByter: Nope, just got the new PC monitor I wanted for gaming.

PillowByter: That was pretty much it.

PillowByter: And my books for next semester.

CircusTent: Every nerd's dream.

PillowByter: Totally.

PillowByter: You must be lost. A jock with no jockstrap.

PillowByter: I'll have to get you one.

CircusTent: What if I did get you something?

PillowByter: Lol. You going to set a trap for me?

PillowByter: Or do you think I'll send you my mailing address?

CircusTent: Worth a shot.

CircusTent: And if I did, it would definitely be a jockstrap.

PillowByter: I'd wear it for you.

CircusTent: Do you have one?

PillowByter: No.

PillowByter: I have three.

CircusTent: Tease.

Once the photo came through – his perfect ass snug in a black micro jock – I replied with one of my hard dick and the conversation took a rather explicit turn.

> PillowByter: That monster would be in my mouth every night.

> CircusTent: Leave the jock on and get my cock nice and slick.

> PillowByter: Can't wait for your full balls to drain themselves all over my face.

> CircusTent: My fingers are prepping your hole.

> PillowByter: I'm ready.

> PillowByter: Fuck me.

I closed my eyes and pumped my fist up and down, tugging my balls with the other hand. In my head, they were slapping Pillow's perfect ass, over and over, but I was close, and the fastest way to orgasm was to pull down on them hard. That increased the sensations along the shaft and made for quicker strokes. My foreskin couldn't slide up and down as easily.

Fuck.

I bit my lip to prevent me inadvertently crying out. All I needed was one of my brothers to come in here channeling their inner Logan and catch me. I was teased enough as a teenager, I didn't need to hear the same stuff as an almost adult.

What I did need was a towel.

My cum rag wasn't something I decided to bring home for the holidays, so a t-shirt would have to suffice. Despite having it, I still made a mess.

> CircusTent: Damn, that was good.

> PillowByter: Did you make a mess?

> CircusTent: Always. You?

PillowByter: Cleaning up now.

> CircusTent: Shirt or washcloth?

PillowByter: Fingers and mouth.

I could've sworn my spent dick twitched on my stomach. After dipping a finger into the few drops of cum that had pooled there, I brought it to my mouth and imagined I was feeding it to him instead.

I wanted to say so much, but I was afraid of killing the fantasy. Was he as cute as his ass was perfect? Would he be as adventurous in person as he was over the phone? Would I?

But these questions were pointless.

It wasn't a formal relationship or anything.

Although we *had* started the regular chat dates.

PillowByter: Too much?

Shit. I was in my head for too long.

> CircusTent: No! Fuck no. You short-circuited my brain.

> CircusTent: You are a sex god.

PillowByter: I try.

I wanted to ask him if he wanted to meet in real life, but I knew what Logan and Danny would say. He's the one that contacted me. Everything had been on his terms so far, and it wouldn't do me any good to push him faster than he wanted.

Unsurprisingly, that t-shirt became very crusty by the end of Christmas break.

· · ·

I couldn't get the idea of meeting him out of my head, so I decided to see if he would take advantage of a relatively empty campus on the off chance that was the reason he was hesitant to reveal himself. Despite my parents' disappointment, I changed my flight and flew back before New Year's Eve.

CircusTent: I'm back.

I waited twenty minutes before heading to the pool. Not only was I addicted to the attention, but I looked forward to any message from him. It certainly felt like what I imagined having a boyfriend to be like.

My head was clear for most of my time in the water, but when I pulled back the throttle and started to relax, thoughts of him returned. I'd only just realized I'd never asked if he had a roommate.

The pool was still empty, but I had been there for just under an hour. I was only getting a head start on training anyway. Coach was fine with us enjoying the holidays because he worked our asses off before them. It was only going to take a week or so to get back to my best condition and move forward.

As soon as I pulled myself out of the pool, I ran through a few of my normal stretches and grabbed a sip from the water fountain. I hadn't bothered with a towel, so I made a quick retreat into the locker room…where a shower was running. I tried to remember which of my teammates was from the Brentwood area, but I couldn't think of any.

"Morning," I said, coming around the corner.

The figure froze, giving me time to admire the almost-full back tattoo of a naked archer. The tattoo was gorgeous and I had to admit the ass was as well. I'd never seen the tattoo before though. *Did we get a new swimmer?*

"Oh fuck!" the young man practically yelped when he turned and saw me.

The exact second I recognized him – "Hayden?!" – his hands

immediately covered his junk, but I had time to tell he was at least partially hard. "So-sorry, I didn't think anyone would be here."

Hayden's head bowed, his eyes on the floor, before he turned to face the wall. He was clearly nervous. "I didn't think anyone would be here either," he said.

"I can go?"

"No, I'm almost done. It's fine."

The silence was awkward, but it didn't last long. I had too many questions. Observations, really.

"I didn't know you had a tattoo. It's so big." I realized that sounded pervy, so I added, "Do you like archery?"

"I know you're naked in front of other guys all the time, Mike, but I'm not and I'm trying really hard not to pass out from embarrassment right now. It's sweet of you to want to chat, but I'm rinsing off and then I'll be going."

"You have nothing to be embarrassed about. Your body is amazing." I wasn't sure my opinion would change his mind, but I had to try. I tried not to be obvious, but he was pretty muscular though I'd never seen him work out. "Not that I'm coming on to you," I added.

His tense back seemed to relax, though it may have been my imagination.

Shit. "Not that I wouldn't come on to you. I mean to say that your body is perfect. More than adequate?"

Finally he rewarded me with a laugh. "I believe you, Mike. You don't forget how to speak around the other guys. I'll take it as a compliment. See you around."

The water shut off and he scurried out of the shower room and around the corner before I could stop him. I was left with more questions than I had before. Like, how did someone so attractive – and to be honest, friendly – feel like they're inadequate?

Maybe he had an ex that treated him like garbage?

I could imagine that would ruin my self-confidence.

Where did all those muscles come from?

That was the more pertinent question.

And that tattoo!

Hayden had an enormous naked man tattooed on his body.

And the semi.

Which reminded me to hurry up and get back to my phone. Maybe I had a message waiting for me. With Logan gone, I could jack it as much as I wanted and not get caught. I dried my wet fingers, draped the towel over my shoulder, and swiped.

PillowByter: You're back?

PillowByter: Back where?

CircusTent: On campus. I came back early.

PillowByter: Any particular reason?

I felt ballsy.

CircusTent: To take you out on a date.

CircusTent: For New Year's.

PillowByter: Oh really?

PillowByter: And what makes you think I'd agree to that after months of remaining anonymous?

CircusTent: The holiday spirit?

PillowByter: LOL. Call me the Grinch.

PillowByter: Maybe I'll get the courage before the end of the semester, but not right now.

PillowByter: Sorry.

CircusTent: It was worth a shot.

It was New Year's Eve, I was out of semen, and campus was deserted. I could've gone into Nashville and found something to occupy my time, but I didn't want to get drunk alone. Finding my way back to campus could be problematic. Plus, there was the chance I wouldn't be served as I was twenty and hadn't bothered with another fake ID since my last one was confiscated.

Since I knew he was around, I took a chance.

> Mike: How's it going?

> Mike: Any plans for tonight?

Plus, part of me wanted to somehow make up for earlier, to show that he could be comfortable around me. I was a little surprised he answered so quickly.

> Hayden: I'm good, and sadly not really.

> Mike: I don't really want to see your dad any sooner than I have to, but maybe I can come over and we can watch the ball drop?

> Mike: I fully realize it's rude to invite oneself over, but my tiny room isn't company-friendly. Plus, there's only so many things I can do by myself and my hand's exhausted.

I stared in horror at the message, realizing I just sent Coach's son a masturbation joke. The seconds felt like minutes. I breathed a sigh of relief when I saw the typing dots bubble on my screen.

> Hayden: Should've asked for a Fleshlight for Christmas.

> Mike: LMAO!

> Hayden: My parents are heading out to a party, so it's just me if you really wanted to hang out.

I deleted the text I was about to send – he was more than enough but I didn't want to patronize him – and retyped.

Mike: What do you like to drink?

Hayden: Honestly?

Mike: Yeah…

Hayden: I like those colorful wine coolers.

Oh. That's kind of cute.
I had them maybe once but it had been a while.

Mike: I can swing that. See you in a bit.

Mike: The white colonial on Carpenter, right?

Hayden: That's the one.

I grabbed my wallet and made for the door, but realized that I hadn't showered all day. Quickly, I stripped, grabbed a towel and my body wash, and headed down the hall.

Soaping up, I thought back to Hayden's Fleshlight joke and as one does, started to harden. I laughed out loud. It never turned off. I should be appreciative of its stamina, but sometimes you just wanted to shower quickly so you could go buy a bunch of fluorescent colored beverages for a friend.

For the booze, I had two options: the big chain store where I might get lost in the crowd, or the small liquor store where the cashier might be the one that flirts with me. I went for option one since it was on the way.

A variety pack of Seagram's Escapes would do for Hayden, and a handful of nips was all I needed, though I'd try Hayden's choice if he let me. I looked for the busiest line as I approached the front, but my eye caught on some familiar wavy brown hair. It was my starry-eyed high schooler from the fall. Tom.

He noticed me before it was my turn and immediately smiled. Every five seconds, he'd glance my way as if to make sure I hadn't run off. And soon enough, it was my turn.

"Hey, Tom."

"You remembered my name?" he said, ringing my items up without looking twice.

I nodded. "Have a good Christmas?"

"It was alright. You?"

"Same."

"Big plans tonight?" he asked before saying the total.

I breathed a sigh of relief. "More like little plans. Hope you don't have to stay too late." I grabbed my purchases before he could answer and rushed out the door.

It only took a few minutes to cross town and find the Sawyer house. Hayden was all smiles when he greeted me at the door. He was wearing gray sweatpants and a faded blue hoodie. I had never seen him so casual.

"Ari!"

"Whoa!" I jumped back, struggling to hold onto the bags.

"Ari, down!" Hayden commanded.

I couldn't help but laugh. "I guess he's feeling better, huh?" Then inwardly cursed myself for not asking sooner.

"Completely recovered," Hayden answered with a smile. "Come inside."

Drunk Hayden was fun.

"I want a blue one."

"We drank all the blue ones," I said. "Pink or green."

"You should have the green. Gimme the pink one."

Pink one isn't quite a euphemism for dick, but it was close enough for two drunk college guys.

"Oh, I'll give you the pink one," I joked, grabbing the crotch of my jeans. All the porn I'd watched earlier made me horny as fuck and now the Seagrams had lowered my self control.

Hayden jumped up on the couch, laughing, and pulled the waistband of his sweats down to reveal baby blue bikini briefs.

"Damn, Hayden, put that away unless you want me to unwrap that package."

Blip.

Hayden froze, causing his pants to slip down his legs. He made a move for his phone on the coffee table, but his legs were trapped together, causing him to fall.

Into my lap. His evidently hard dick pressed against my thigh, his pert butt right in front of my face. Instinctively, I cupped a cheek.

He scrambled off me, pulling his pants up and reaching his phone.

"Is he cute?"

"Wh-what? Who?"

"The guy on Grindr."

"Uh…that's actually my boyfriend," Hayden replied.

"Your boyfriend's on Grindr?"

Hayden laughed. "Uh, no. He changed the sound on my phone to the Grindr noise as a joke."

My alcohol-infused brain accepted that as funny, but I started to wonder what his boyfriend looked like. I was a little jealous.

First the tattoo. Then the magnificent ass. Not to mention he was so easy to talk to.

"I'm empty!" Hayden said, before heading into the kitchen. "Need another?"

I downed what I had left in three swallows. "Yeah!"

Hayden returned with two more bottles. "Last ones, then it's the nips."

Of course I had to lift my shirt up and tweak my nipples for that, which almost made him drop the bottles.

"So where's this boyfriend of yours?" I made myself comfortable on one end of the couch. Ari was curled up on the floor in front of us.

"Another school?" Hayden answered, sitting farther away from me than before.

"It sounds like you're making him up," I challenged.

"Why would I do that?"

"To keep me away from your ass."

Hayden rolled his eyes. "You are so drunk right now."

I heard a door slam and someone said they were home, but I was so out of it, I barely opened my eyes.

"I don't want to know." Coach Sawyer was standing there, his hands on his hips. "Good night, boys."

CHAPTER 8

"So you woke up and his face was snuggled up against your junk?"

"Yup."

"What happened next? You poke him awake with your dick?" Logan asked.

We were catching each other up on our holiday break adventures. Logan was being evasive about his vacation, but I was sharing every detail.

"Nothing really happened. He played it off on the alcohol and made me breakfast, then I came back here, showered and took a nap."

"I think you missed a golden opportunity, man. You pretty much had a romantic evening and then cuddled all night *and* he made you breakfast. Now you're telling me all about it as if it wasn't a big deal."

"Because it wasn't." I shoved him, but he barely moved. "He has a boyfriend!"

"Oh yeah, this mysterious *boyfriend*." Logan made sure to add air quotes to emphasize his point. "He's either imaginary or he's a terrible boyfriend. Who leaves their boyfriend alone on New Year's Eve?"

"Moving on to the other man in my life." I waved my phone. Luckily, Logan took the bait.

"How is the supreme bottom boy, biter-of-the-pillow these days?"

"He's been quiet ever since I mentioned wanting to meet up again. I think I scared him off."

Logan shook his head. "Spice things up with a dick pic?"

Hmm. "That's not a bad idea. You mind leaving the room?"

"Like you don't have a curated album of perfectly-lit shafts that look three inches bigger than reality all prepared to send." Logan scoffed. "I'll be happy to take a new one for you. Let me just get the studio ready."

Logan was right. A rando dick pic wasn't a good idea; it really was all about the lighting. There were a few I hadn't sent to Pillow yet.

It was hard to admit, but I was nervous waiting for his response.

> PillowByter: I can't believe you walk around with that every day.

I smiled, then typed.

> CircusTent: Do I hide it well?

> PillowByter: Not that I'm staring…

> PillowByter: But yes.

> PillowByter: Definitely a grower.

> PillowByter: What do you feed that monster?

> CircusTent: Promises of a nice, tight hole like yours.

> PillowByter: Only if you treat it like a prince.

I was glad our hypersexual banter was back.

CircusTent: I'd definitely introduce it to my tongue.

CircusTent: Would you like that?

PillowByter: Hmm…a hot jock tongue-fucking me?

PillowByter: If I'm gonna take that beast, I'm gonna need to be loosened up.

CircusTent: You cum first.

PillowByter: Can I cum now?

CircusTent: Can you cum now, what?

PillowByter: Can I cum now, sir?

"I can see you're horny, so I'll leave you to it."

I glanced up to see Logan's smirk before he left our room, then glanced down where I had been absent-mindedly touching myself. There was a massive tent in my shorts and I laughed.

I switched to Messages and fired off a quick text.

Mike: The dick wants what the dick wants.

Logan: You're lucky I love you like a brother.

Logan: Have fun.

Then swiped back to Grindr.

CircusTent: Get on your hands and knees.

I was furiously stroking my cock and about to cum when-

Danny: Practice is about to start.

Danny: Where are you?

Fuck.

PillowByter: Your balls are so tight.

PillowByter: So full.

CircusTent: I'm so sorry.

CircusTent: I'm late for practice. I completely forgot.

CircusTent: Cum raincheck.

I grabbed my gym bag and ran out the door. I could feel my hard dick bouncing in my shorts, but I didn't care. Maybe someone would enjoy the view?

Jesus Christ! Why didn't I change?! It was freezing out.

Coach was going to be pissed. It was the first practice after the holidays. My bike lock took longer to unlock than normal because I was rushing and fucked up the combo. I almost got hit by a car that I didn't see, or rather I wasn't even looking because I was trying to avoid students and curbs and trees.

The brush with death killed my erection, so as I burst into the locker room, I didn't have that to worry about. Not that anyone noticed. It was empty.

Tearing off my hoodie and tossing it into my locker, I unzipped my bag to find...a towel, a jockstrap and my gym clothes.

Shit.

I pulled the hoodie back out of the locker and looked for a Speedo. Nothing.

God damn it.

"Hayden?" I called out for help. He'd have the team's competition suits, but no one answered. I jogged over to the closet, searching past the towels and found bins with Speedos in them.

Racing back to my locker, I stripped, pulled up the swim briefs and ran out to the pool.

"Ramsey! Get your ass over here!"

Just as the chlorine scent hit my sinuses was when I realized my error, but it was too late. I just needed to take Coach's verbal lashing and get in the water. Maybe no one would notice?

"What are you wearing?"

So much for no one noticing.

"I mean- Shit, sorry. Is this why you're late? You forgot your suit and couldn't find something in your size?"

Glancing down, I could see my pubes sprawled over the top of the suit. "Sorry, Coach. Hayden wasn't there and I just grabbed one and rushed out."

"Yeah, he's late, too."

"Nice ass, Mike. I didn't know the sun was out?"

"What?" I turned to see Danny smiling from the side of the pool.

"You know…because your buns are out."

I reached behind me and could feel a few inches of my butt crack was exposed. *Fuuuck.*

"Do you want to go find another one?"

"No, I'd like to just get in the water, sir."

"Suit yourself. Just to let you know I was prepared to punish you with extra laps"–Coach smiled–"but I think your teammates will punish you enough."

As if on cue, the wolf whistles started, followed by verbal teasing, led by Danny, that left me red in the face. I hurried to move past Coach, but the door to the locker room opened and Hayden ran straight into my chest.

"So-sorry," he stammered, before dashing around me. "I fell asleep, Dad. Sorry."

I heard Coach ask Hayden to make sure the locker room bins were labeled properly. When I paused to figure out what Coach meant, I saw him pointing at me and Hayden's eyes went wide. He had seen what the rest of the team had: my ass bulging out of the top of my skimpy Speedo.

I dove into the pool and immediately swam to Danny to attempt to drown him.

There were two advantages to a swimsuit that was too small for me. There was no room for my dick to harden from all the attention, and it was so tight it wasn't going to fall off. Ever.

Despite not getting extra laps from Coach, I decided to stay a little later and do a little more on my own. Danny stayed too, teasing me on the way to the locker room that he just needed to see the tiny briefs up close.

"Shut the fuck up. You've seen me naked, multiple times."

"Yeah, but that is like a kid's Speedo. How did you not notice when you put it on? It looks so tight."

Danny held the door open for me.

"Fine! There! Happy?!" I yelled before yanking it down and throwing it to the side.

Slap.

"Whoa."

"Oh my God, I'm so sorry!" I ran over to Hayden who had just been mauled in the face with my wet Speedo.

"It's okay," he said as we both pulled it off at the same time. However, the Speedo remained in his hands.

We both seemed to notice I was completely naked and inches from his body at the same time.

Danny cleared his throat, causing me to look at him. "Shower, Mikey?"

"Uh, yeah." I apologized again and broke eye contact with Hayden, who turned and disappeared into the laundry room.

"Did you need a moment?" Danny whispered.

"What do you mean?"

"You and Hayden just now."

"I just threw a wet Speedo in his face. What was I supposed to do? Ignore him?"

Danny shrugged. "Just seemed like something. That's all."

"It's probably because we spent New Year's together."

Danny paused his soaping to stare at me. "Say what?"

I walked over to the lockers, careful not to slip, to see if Hayden had left and I didn't see him. Back under the stream of hot water, I spent the entire shower replaying the entire night for Danny. We were both prunes by the time all his questions were answered. He was as bad as Logan.

"Man, you are just a snack, aren't you?" Danny teased, squeezing my bicep.

"I told you-"

"Oh, I know. 'Hayden has a boyfriend.' By the way, I agree with Logan. Smells like a lie. But even if he does, which I *doubt*, I think it's obvious he likes you. Maybe things don't work out?" Danny suggested.

"What about my secret admirer?"

"A bird in the hand, or should I say cock?" He grabbed his junk through his towel and winked.

"You and Logan should just fuck," I replied, knowing that would shut him up. Walking between the rows of lockers, I headed to mine. "What? No smart retort?" I asked, looking back at Danny.

"Fine." Danny stopped to put his hands on his hips. "How about you message your Grindr boy right now then? Especially since you left him mid-coitus."

He had a point. I grabbed my phone from my duffle bag.

> CircusTent: Sorry about that.

Blip.

"What'd he say?" Danny asked.

"That wasn't my phone."

"What do you mean? No one else is in here."

CircusTent: Hope you held off for me.

Blip.

"It's coming from this bag," Danny said, pushing it into view with his bare foot. It was one of those reusable bags from Whole Foods.

"Maybe it's a coincidence?"

"Try sending three in a row and we'll see." Danny sat down next to me.

CircusTent: I hope

Blip.

CircusTent: you're still

Blip.

CircusTent: horny.

Blip.

"Oh my God! It's Pillow's phone!" Danny half-screamed.

"That means he *is* a teammate," I said. "Should we look in the bag?"

"I mean, we *need* to return it to its owner. Phones are expensive," Danny reasoned. "And he's missing all his Grindr messages."

I couldn't help it. My hands were shaking as I peeked in the bag.

"Well, what's in it?" Danny asked.

"I can't see the phone. There's some other stuff. Am I supposed to just dig through all of it?"

"How else are we going to find clues?"

I took a deep breath and kept looking.

"Some shorts, a shirt."

"What's on it?"

"Mack Swimming," I answered, tossing it to him. "A jockstrap."

"Really?"

I pulled it out to show him. It was one of those designer ones. Not for swimming or working out. It said Pump on it.

"Nice quality. Never heard of the brand though," Danny said.

"Here's the phone." The screen came alive as I touched it. "Oh!"

"What?" Danny sat next to me, the colorful jockstrap still in his hands.

I handed him the phone. "I know who Pillow is."

"Cute dog, but whose is it?"

CHAPTER 9

n the end, I made Danny return the bag to Hayden. I was overwhelmed.

I had sent those messages as a test and Hayden was smart. He'd figure out what I did and be embarrassed and probably clam up like he'd done so many other times. I didn't want things to end up like that. I didn't want him to feel awkward, I wanted him to be happy.

And take his clothes off.

With me.

I swore Logan to secrecy, but his mind was blown when I revealed Pillow's identity. He wanted me to buy some flowers, ride down to the Sawyers' house, and ask him out immediately.

I wasn't going to do that.

I told Logan I'd handle it and then suggested that maybe he focus on his cam sex relationship instead of mine.

· · ·

Now that I knew, it was obvious. At practice, I'd glance his way and half the time he was already looking at me. It became a little game, trying to catch him.

"You should message him on Grindr when you can watch him react," Danny suggested.

"If I do that, he's going to look directly at me, and I won't be able to watch his reaction because he'll see me watching him and then he'll know I know."

"Oh brother. He probably already knows you know."

The locker room was even worse. I couldn't help but put on a show. I made sure to spend extra time lathering my balls or my ass, especially when he was around. With my eyes closed and head back, of course – torso on full display.

I stopped doing that the day I heard a loud metallic bang. Hayden had walked into the lockers and landed on his ass on the floor. I ran over to try to help him, but slipped myself. I had forgotten that water and soap didn't create the best surface for running.

I felt arms pick me up from behind. "You two alright?" It was Danny.

"I'm good, thanks," I answered.

"Just my body getting in the way. I'm okay," Hayden replied, then disappeared around the corner.

"When are you revealing yourself?" Danny whispered.

"Is this not revealing enough?"

Danny rolled his eyes. "Not what I meant. And he's seen that a hundred times by now."

"I'm waiting for a special day."

I was waiting for Valentine's Day to be exact.

My attempts at real life shenanigans were nothing compared to our Grindr chats now. Knowing who it was on the other end of the conversation was so much hotter. I had known Hayden for almost two years and lately – whether it was pure luck or not – we had spent some time together. He was definitely boyfriend material, and if our Grindr conversations were any indication, we were sexually compatible too.

Part of me was nervous things wouldn't work in person, but part of me knew I needed to try. He was worth that, and he obviously liked me. It was hard to imagine him as the same person from the beginning.

Harpocrates.

Of course he hadn't changed, I just got to know him a lot better, which only made me like him more.

A few days prior I got with Coach and reserved the pool, but the big day was finally here.

> Mike: Can you meet me at the pool?

> Hayden: Sure…everything okay?

> Mike: I came for a swim and the door to the locker room won't open.

> Mike: I can't get back in and I don't want to use the emergency exit. Speedos and snow don't mix.

> Mike: I thought you might have keys?

Logan had come up with that excuse. Just enough reason that he needed to come, but not outrageously fake.

> Hayden: Yeah, I can be there in fifteen minutes or so.

> Mike: Great! You're a lifesaver. I owe you whatever you want.

I couldn't help throwing a little flirt his way. We were finally going to meet.

I was busy lighting candles when the notification from Door-

Dash popped – dinner was here. After tipping the delivery driver and closing the app, I scurried back through the building and over to the table I had set up poolside. The silverware I borrowed from the dining hall was already on the table, so I just had to slide napkins underneath and pull everything out of the bag. A quick trip to the trash can by the door and all I had left to do was finish the candles and turn off the overhead lights.

"Mike?" Hayden's voice echoed through the dimly-lit natatorium. "Oh my God."

I stood smiling next to the table, illuminated by the hundreds of floating candles in the pool behind me. "Good evening and happy Valentine's Day."

"What is all this?" he asked, approaching me. "You weren't locked in, were you?"

I shook my head, took a deep breath for courage and grabbed his hand. He didn't pull away, so I squeezed and led him towards the table.

"This is all for you, Hayden. If you take a seat, I think your place card will reveal what you need to know."

"My place card?"

I pulled the chair out from the table and waited for him to sit. While I made my way around the table, he must've read it because he asked, "When did you know?"

"That you bite pillows?" I took my seat, grabbing the napkin to put on my lap.

"I'm assuming it had something to do with Danny finding my phone?"

"See, you're a smart boy." I winked. "And yes. I messaged you on Grindr and the phone went off in the locker room."

"You've known for...almost a month?! I should've known. All those fucking flirty glances. Every time I looked at you, you were looking at me."

"Trust me, I noticed too, and we were connecting in real life *and* on Grindr, so don't get mad at me for liking it. I was hypnotized that you could be that dirty. You're usually so reserved."

"Well"–he took a sip of his water–"maybe I'm saving it for the bedroom?"

"I bet you are," I said, a huge smile plastered on my face. "And you're not really saving anything. I've seen practically every part of you."

"I can't believe you did all this for me," Hayden said, gesturing to the pool.

"It's like I knew you'd appreciate a grand gesture. You're kind of a romantic, you know?"

"I...am aware. How did you know I liked this place?"

He was referring to the meal from Gino's currently plated in front of him. I shrugged. "When I was at your house for New Year's, I saw the paper bags by the recycling. I figured I'd give it a shot."

"Well, your observational skills paid off. It's my favorite place."

I screamed a huge congratulations to myself inside my head and flashed a smile. "It's really good. I didn't happen to guess your favorite dish, did I?"

Hayden shook his head. "I like the Italian sampler, but this is up there," he said, before taking another bite. "Wait a minute, what about my boyfriend?"

"Your fake boyfriend?"

Hayden smiled. "I suppose that was a little transparent. I'm not a good liar."

"To be fair, I had no idea...for a long time. But once I knew it was you, I didn't think you'd be messaging me on Grindr and leaving me notes if you had a boyfriend."

Hayden nodded, then asked, "What did you order?"

"Cheese ravioli," I answered. "I like my pasta stuffed."

"Like you like your men."

"Hopefully."

The tension was thick. Now that it was all on the table, it seemed nothing was off limits.

"Are we going for a swim later?" Hayden asked.

"We can, but I didn't bring a Speedo."

"There's some in the locker room," Hayden suggested.

"I don't think I want to do that again."

Hayden laughed, but kept his eyes on mine. "My dad would kill us if we got caught."

"Let's not get caught then."

We kept eating while the conversation varied between us reliving our entire relationship from the moment I received the first note to small talk about our current lives. His enormous back tattoo was of special interest to me, as it had remained a secret the entire time we had known each other. His reply was he didn't live as shirtless an existence as I did.

I practically fell out of my chair when I felt pressure on my crotch.

"Easy, tiger," Hayden purred. "I'll be gentle."

"Jesus." I closed my eyes. *How can someone's toes be so talented?*

"Hmm…feels about as big as it should."

I had to put my fork down. As if I could eat anyway. I was rock hard and completely uninterested in anything on the table. "If you keep doing that, I don't think we'll be doing much swimming."

Hayden smiled and the footjob ended. I immediately regretted saying anything.

"Oh, your ass is getting in that pool, Mike. I already know what I want for dessert."

"I can't believe you're finally letting go," I said, a little surprised at his forwardness.

"You did the hard part for me, Mike."

Fuck.

Hayden, without any hesitation, stood up, turned around – his ass was even better in person – stripped and dove into the pool. I wasn't about to ignore what amounted to an invitation to, at the very least, skinny-dip with my closet-hot secret admirer.

I took my clothes off as fast as I could and went to slide into the pool – I didn't want to disturb any more of the candles – but Hayden's hands on my thighs stopped me and his mouth immediately engulfed my entire cock.

"Shouldn't we – oh fuck! – discuss our sexual…histories?"

The slurp as he pulled off practically echoed. "Are you really asking me if I've tested while you're about to be blown?"

"Yes?"

Hayden laughed. "Okay, I can respect that. I haven't been with anyone since my high school boyfriend," he answered. "So it's been a few years for me and my test last year was negative. What about you?"

"I'm, uh…a virgin."

"Seriously? I get to take your cherry? Fuck, that's so hot."

"You're okay with that?"

"Okay?! More than okay, Mike. I'm a little surprised since your sex talk is absolutely filthy."

"All thanks to porn, I assure you," I said.

"But we can do whatever you want. Just tell me and it's yours."

"Your mouth felt pretty good?"

Hayden shook his head. "Pretty good? That just won't do. Close your eyes and relax."

I did as he said, bracing myself with my hands behind me. His hands grabbed my thighs again and I felt his tongue swirl around my balls before making its way up the shaft to engulf the head. Up and down, over and over, I was lost in it. He'd change the suction, then he'd change the speed, then he'd use a hand and jack me off at the same time.

"You're so good"–I managed to speak–"at this, Hayden."

"I love hearing you say my name."

I liked to hear that, but I knew this needed to stop soon or my boys would be landing in the chlorine in a few seconds. "Hold up." I put a hand on his shoulder. "Let's take this into the locker room."

"What's in there?" Hayden asked.

"Lube, for starters," I answered.

"And what are we gonna do with that?" he asked, giving the head of my glistening cock another lick.

"I'm gonna make you scream my name."

Had anyone interrupted the clean-up of the candles in the pool via nets or the rushed takedown of the dining set, they would've seen two muscular, completely naked men scurrying around the deck with bouncing erections, and I would've died from embarrassment. Luckily, no one found us and the locker room was as deserted as the pool.

"This is going to be quick," I warned.

"We have time for a slow fuck later. I just want to cum with you inside of me."

I headed for my locker to grab the lube.

"Where do you want me?" Hayden asked.

"Bend over. Put your hands on the bench."

He did as commanded, then I heard him say, "I can't believe this is finally happening."

Just hearing that he had imagined this, had waited for this, made my dick harder. He hissed when I drizzled the lube onto his crack. I quickly apologized then dipped a finger into the clear fluid and slowly trailed it down until I brushed his hole.

"Fuck, that feels good."

"You ready?"

"Finger me first. You've got a huge dick. You're gonna need to prep me."

"Okay. Just tell me if I'm doing it wrong."

"It's pretty simple. One finger, then two. Keep adding lube."

I was amazed to see that he had a completely hairless ass. With my other hand, I squeezed his plump cheek and felt no stubble. It was natural. Spreading his cheeks apart, I finally saw his little, pink rosebud. It was wet already from the initial lube, but I wanted to make it good for him, so I added more.

"Oh fuck." Hayden groaned.

"That okay?" I was afraid this was all wrong.

"Jesus Christ, yes. More. More, please."

He didn't have to ask me again. I switched hands and used the leftover lube to slick up my cock, making sure to get under my foreskin.

"How many is that? It feels so good."

"Three," I answered, pulling out just a little to add more lube.

"That's enough. I need you to fuck me now."

I grabbed the lube, squirted more on my cock, and guided it towards his hole. With a hand on Hayden's back, I slowly pushed inside. It felt so tight…and warm. Unlike anything I'd ever felt.

"Fuck. How much of it is in?"

I glanced down. "Maybe half?"

"Add more lube and give me a few seconds."

I did as instructed. "All set?"

"Yeah."

In a few seconds, I was all the way in. "That's it."

"Trust me, that is anything but it. It's fantastic is what it is. I'm good. You can go for it now."

Slowly, I pulled out and slid it back in. I didn't know what I expected, but it wasn't this. This was a thousand times better.

"You can go harder. I can take it now."

I grabbed his hips and the sound of my body slamming into his filled the locker room, as did the expletives coming out of his mouth.

"Are you close? I'm close," I said. "Fuck, that's embarrassing."

"Wait, wait, wait. Let's switch positions." Hayden stood up and moved forward, my cock slid out of his body.

"Holy shit, that felt weird."

"Well, for me it feels like I'm being split open. In a good way, of course." Hayden grabbed a towel from my locker and laid it on the bench. After straddling it, he laid back and held his legs in the air. "Have at it, big top."

I caught his jab and threw it back at him. "Maybe you can bite the towel since there aren't any pillows here?"

"Less talk, more cock."

"I knew you'd be a bossy bottom," I said, grabbing his ankles.

Hayden reached over his head to grab the bench to steady himself. "Get to it-ahhh! Fuck!"

After a few minutes of pumping, I was close again. Hayden had started jacking himself as I fucked him. He grabbed my ass, pulling me into him. "I'm close! Fuck!"

I lost myself in the moment. I became a machine, pistoning in and out. The slapping sound of my legs against his ass was such a turn-on.

"I want you to breed me!" Hayden yelled. "I can't believe I just said that."

"It's all – good – fuck!" At this point, I was channeling all the porn I had ever watched. Every movement I mimicked, every phrase I copied, and I didn't care how it sounded. "Take my cock, boy. I'm gonna fill you up."

Hayden's hips bucked. "Cumming!"

I watched as the first spurt launched from his dick and as soon as his hole clenched around my cock, I lost it. "Me too!" My eyes closed as the orgasm washed over me. Each pump came slower than the last and the locker room grew quieter.

All I could hear eventually was the sound of our heavy breathing.

"Best Valentine's Day ever," Hayden said, cum dripping from his chin.

I had to agree.

ACKNOWLEDGMENTS

I'd like to thank the following people for their help with this short story: Raquel, Jess, Nedra, Katey, Brandon, Nicole, Wren, Kristy, and Elizabeth. Additionally, this story couldn't have happened without Lee Blair, the creator and organizer of the Candy Hearts Anthology. She was such an organized, cheerful, and focused project manager — thank you for including me.

ALSO BY FINN DIXON

RINGS TRILOGY & CHAMPIONS SERIES

Rings of Lust

Floored by Love

The Forever Vault

Dickathlon

SNOW DATES SERIES

Snowballing

Jack Frosting

North Pole Dancer

OTHER WORKS

Camp Jackwood

Frat Ghost Wingman

ABOUT THE AUTHOR

Finn Dixon made a childhood dream come true and has worked in the zoological field since 2006. He's taken care of everything from alligators to zebras, but his favorites will always be rhinos. Thus far, his MM romances have focused on contemporary stories that include jocks (and jockstraps), but fantasy, paranormal, and historical have been observed in the crystal ball of Finn's future.

If you liked Mike and Hayden, you'll find the same heart and humor with the Champions guys. He hopes you'll give them a chance.

In his spare time, he likes watching gay films and shows with happy endings (giggity), playing Disney Dreamlight Valley, re-watching Jurassic Park and Clue, and traveling when he can afford it. If you'd like to keep up with the latest Finn Dixon has to offer, check him out on Instagram or FinnDixonWriting.com. You can also join the beasties in his private Facebook group, Finn Dixon's MMenagerie, on Discord, and the MM Wire on The Circle.

And yes, he likes jocks, but he promises all his books won't be about them.

Or will they?

For future news and updates,
subscribe to his newsletter by going to the website below.
www.finndixonwriting.com